CHLOE THE CAMPERVAN'S ADVENTURES IN RHYME

Chloe Goes to the Zoo

Written and Illustrated by Brian Prescott

Chloe Goes To The Zoo

First published 2014 by Beaten Track Publishing

A CIP catalogue record for this book
is available from the British Library.

ISBN: 978 1 909192 53 9

Beaten Track Publishing,
Burscough. Lancashire.
www.beatentrackpublishing.com

Beaten Track

CHLOE THE CAMPERVAN'S ADVENTURES IN RHYME

Chloe Goes to the Zoo

“It’s time for me to get up;
“There are lots of things to do.
“Then later on this morning,
“We’re going to the zoo.”

CHLOE

"I'm meeting Percy Pick-Up,
"Just outside the gate.
"He's buying me my ticket,
"So I'd better not be late."

ZOO. WAY IN
ZOO. WAY IN
TO
CHLOE
PERCY

The weather's nice, the crowds are out.
There are lots of things to see.
Elephants and a tiger,
And a monkey in a tree.

ELEPHANTS
TIGERS
LITTE

A seal and penguins swimming,
And putting on a show,
And parrots riding bicycles—
"Who taught them? I don't know!"

At all these clever animals,
They couldn't help but laugh,
But then they heard a worried shout...
"Have you seen my giraffe?"

GIRAFFE HOUSE
ZOO

The keeper's in a panic;
"Jim has got out through the gate!"
"We will have to help him find Jim,
"Before it gets too late."

ICE CREAM
WAY OUT
ELEPHANTS
PERCY
GIRAFFES
CHLOE

Eventually they found him,
Too tired to even talk.
“We’ll have to help Jim home,” said Perce,
“’cause he isn’t fit to walk.”

GIRAFFE HOUSE
PERCY
CHLOE
P

"Thank you!" said the keeper,
"For going out of your way,
"Not only did you rescue Jim...
"You also SAVED THE DAY!"

PERCY
CHLOE

ZOO
THE END
CHLOE

Lightning Source UK Ltd.
Milton Keynes UK
UKIC01n1949180314
228328UK00002B/3
* 9 7 8 1 9 0 9 1 9 2 5 3 9 *